WINGS

A Tale of Two Chickens

JAMES MARSHALL

◆

PUFFIN BOOKS

For Muriel Korn

PUFFIN BOOKS

Viking Penguin Inc., 40 West 23rd Street, New York, New York 10010, U.S.A.
Penguin Books Ltd, 27 Wrights Lane, London W8 5TZ (Publishing & Editorial) and
Harmondsworth, Middlesex, England (Distribution & Warehouse)
Penguin Books Australia Ltd, Ringwood, Victoria, Australia
Penguin Books Canada Limited, 2801 John Street, Markham, Ontario, Canada L3R 1B4
Penguin Books (N.Z.) Ltd, 182–190 Wairau Road, Auckland 10, New Zealand

First published by Viking Penguin Inc., 1986
Published in Puffin Books 1988
Copyright © James Marshall, 1986
All rights reserved
Printed in Japan by Dai Nippon Printing Co. Ltd.
Set in Garamond #3

Library of Congress Cataloging-in-Publication Data
Marshall, James
Wings : a tale of two chickens. Summary: Harriet the chicken rescues her foolish friend from the
clutches of a wily fox. [1. Friendship—Fiction. 2. Chickens—Fiction. 3. Animals—
Fiction] I. Title.
PZ7.M35672Wk 1988 [E] 87-20499
ISBN 0-14-050579-2

That evening Harriet put Winnie to bed with a good book.
"Oh, my stars!" cried Winnie. "Mr. Johnson was a *fox!*"
And she nearly died of fright.

"Maybe there's hope for her yet," said Harriet.

"You have caused me a lot of trouble,"
said the plump gray fox.
"Now help me out of this embarrassing costume!"

Winnie was so surprised, she nearly fell out of the balloon.
"Harriet!" she cried. "*You!*"

At that moment, Mr. Johnson's balloon floated by.
The plump gray fox threw Winnie into the basket,
jumped in after her,

and they were gone.
Mr. Johnson was fit to be tied.

"Unhand that chicken!" he cried. "She's mine!"

Soon they found themselves at the edge of a steep cliff.
"Phooey!" said the plump gray fox. "We'll have to turn back."

"Oh, lookee," said Winnie. "Here comes nice Mr. Johnson."
And Mr. Johnson was almost upon them.

The plump gray fox took Winnie by the wing,
and they slipped out the back door.

"Are we playing a game?" said Winnie.
"Just run!" said the fox.

"I didn't see any sardines," said Winnie.
"What's this?" cried the preacher.

"Chicken stealing is wicked!"
Mr. Johnson tore out of the church.

"And what have we here?" said the preacher.
"Two kind souls have brought a bag of food
to share with the poor."

"No! No!" cried Mr. Johnson.
"Be generous!" cried the preacher.
And the bag ripped open.

Inside, the preacher was talking about charity.
"It is our duty to help the needy," he said.

"Humpf," muttered Mr. Johnson.

At Three Corners it began to rain.
Nothing worse than plucking soggy feathers, thought Mr. Johnson.
"Shall we take shelter at this church?" he suggested.

They loaded the bag onto the bicycle and rode away.

"What is in the bag?" asked the plump gray fox.
"My laundry," said Mr. Johnson.

"May I be of some assistance?"
said a plump gray fox.

"I'd be ever so grateful," said Mr. Johnson.

"If at first you don't succeed…" said Mr. Johnson.
But he soon found the bag was quite heavy.

Just then he heard the sound of bicycle tires on dry leaves.

"Care for some sardines?" said Mr. Johnson,
opening his big burlap bag.
"Oooh," said Winnie. "I *love* sardines."

"In you go!" said Mr. Johnson.

Mr. Johnson couldn't believe his luck.
"Is this where chickens cross over?" said Winnie.
"Indeed it is," said Mr. Johnson.

"Travel makes me *so* hungry," said Winnie.

So, wearing his clever new disguise, he went to a place where chickens were known to cross the road.

"Hee-hee," he said. "They'll think I'm one of them."

"Yoo-hoo," said a voice.

Meanwhile, Mr. Johnson hadn't given up hope
of a chicken dinner.
"A chicken costume?" said the clerk in the costume store.

"You heard me," said Mr. Johnson.

But Winnie was soon bored.
And she left the balloon
at the nearest water tower.
"I'll ask folks around here
how to get home,"
she said.

Winnie decided to make herself more comfortable.
"I'll just get rid of these useless old sandbags," she said.

Mr. Johnson came out just in time
to see the balloon heading south.

Mr. Johnson made an unscheduled stop.
"I'll be right back," he said, rushing into a grocery store.
"Quick!" he told the grocer.
"I need a package of instant dumplings!"

Harriet went to the cops.
"We'll do our best," said the officer,
"but foxes *are* clever."
"We'll see about that," said Harriet.

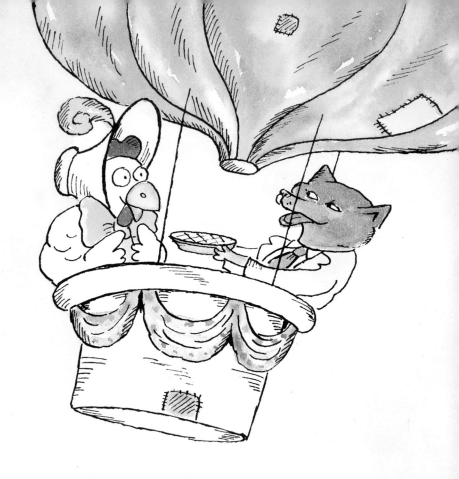

The stranger introduced himself as Mr. Johnson.

"Have a raspberry tart," he said.

"I don't want to get too plump," said Winnie.

"Plump is nice," said Mr. Johnson.

"She never did have a lick of sense,"
said the neighbors.

"Didn't she *know* it was a fox?"
"She never reads," said Harriet.

But it was too late.
"I'll be back for dinner!"
shouted Winnie.
And they were gone.

"Why not?" said Winnie.
And she climbed up the ladder and into the basket.
"Blast off!" cried the stranger.
"Stop! Stop!" cried Harriet.

"My, my," said Winnie.

"Care to go for a spin?" said the stranger.
"Oh, I couldn't," said Winnie.
"Oh, come on," said the stranger.
"Live a little."

One afternoon, Winnie was wandering in the garden.
"Nothing really wild ever happens around here," she said.
"Good afternoon," said a silky voice.
But there was no one there.

"Look up!" said the voice.

Many interesting hobbies kept Harriet busy all day.

"I'm so bored I could just die," said Winnie.

Harriet was enormously fond of reading.

"Frankly, I'd rather swat flies," said Winnie.

Harriet and Winnie were as different
as two chickens could possibly be.